D1365796

Rainy Days with Bear

Written by
Maureen Hull

Illustrated by
Leanne Franson

Lobster Press ™

Rainy Days with Bear
Text © 2004 Maureen Hull
Illustrations © 2004 Leanne Franson

All rights reserved. No part of this publication may be reproduced, stored in any retrieval system or transmitted, in any form or by any means, without the prior written permission of Lobster Press™.

Published by
Lobster Press™
1620 Sherbrooke Street West, Suites C & D
Montréal, Québec   H3H 1C9
Tel. (514) 904-1100 • Fax (514) 904-1101
www.lobsterpress.com

Publisher: Alison Fripp
Editors: Alison Fripp & Karen Li
Book Design: Lorna Mulligan
Cover Design & Production: Tammy Desnoyers

We acknowledge the financial support of the Government of Canada through the Book Publishing Industry Development Program (BPIDP) for our publishing activities.

The Canada Council | Le Conseil des Arts
for the Arts | du Canada

We acknowledge the support of the Canada Council for the Arts for our publishing program.

National Library of Canada Cataloguing in Publication

Hull, Maureen, 1949-
    Rainy days with bear / Maureen Hull ; illustrated by Leanne Franson.

ISBN 1-894222-85-7

    I. Franson, Leanne II. Title.

PS8565.U542R34 2004   jC813'.54   C2003-905916-2

Printed and bound in Hong Kong.

For Amy, Anna, Christopher, Cordelia, Moira, Rebecca and Ryan.

– Maureen Hull

"For the Pamela Jane Onion Boy who is mine forever."

– Leanne Franson

It rained every day for weeks. Bear was not happy.

"Let's take a trip," he said. "To Trinidad."
"I'm too busy," I said. "I have to finish writing this book."

"I need to go to Trinidad
to learn to play steel drums,"
said Bear.

"Go in your imagination,"
I said.

Bear went to the kitchen. He banged on the pots and pans.

He made a lot of noise.

The next day it rained again.

"I know," said Bear, "let's go to Spain and dance the Flamenco."

"I can't," I said. "You made too much noise yesterday. I didn't get any writing done."

Bear went down to the basement and practiced flamenco dancing.

"*Olé!*" he shouted. He stamped his feet very fast.

"Bear," I said the next day, "no foot stamping today."
"Too noisy?" he asked.
"Yes," I said.

An hour later I heard a strange noise.

It went **on** and **on**,

LoudeR

And

LouDeR.

Bear was standing on the couch. He was blowing into a long tube made of paper towel rolls stuck together.
"I'm on the Swiss Alps," he said. "This is my alpine horn."

"Where are the paper towels that were on those rolls?" I asked.

"In the kitchen," he said. "On the floor."

"Are you going to pick them up?" I asked.

"Yes," he said. "When I get back from Switzerland."

The next day it rained again.
"Are you finished yet?" Bear looked over my shoulder.
"No," I said. "Still writing."

Bear went downstairs.
He made a strange huffing,
humming noise.

I ran after him.

"Bear!" I yelled.
"Are you choking?
Can you speak?"

"Of course," he said. "I'm throat-singing. I'm in the Arctic."
"You don't sound like a throat-singer," I said.
"We should go to the Arctic," said Bear, "I need lessons."

"Why is the dog tied to the chair?" I asked.
"That's my dogsled," said Bear. "After I finish singing I'm going dogsledding."

The next day the sun shone for one minute.

Then the rain came back.

"It will never stop," said Bear. "The ocean will be everywhere."

"Pretend you're at the beach," I said.
Bear put on sunglasses. He played "Ukulele Lady"
on his ukulele.
"*Aloha,*" I said.

The next day Bear stayed in bed.

"It's too rainy to get up," he said.

"Go to pretend-Trinidad and bang on the pots," I said. "I won't mind a little noise."

"I did that," he said. He pulled the covers over his head.

"I can't do it again. I'm too sad."

I went to the store.
I got honey ice cream and
a video about Russia.

I let Bear eat the ice cream and
watch the video in bed.

When I checked in to see how he was, he was dancing. His arms were folded. He was kicking his legs in the air and yelling, "*Hup! Hup! Hup!*"

The next day, *I* was sad. "It's too rainy to write," I said.
"Too bad the ice cream is gone," said Bear. "But I can tell you a joke.
How many bears do you need to change a lightbulb?"
"I don't know."

"*Bear*-ly any!"

"Knock, knock," he said.

"Who's there?"

"Bear."

"Bear who?"

"Owls say whoooo. Bears say *grrrrrrrrrrrrrrrrr.*" He jumped on me and tickled me.

    "Thanks," I said. "I feel better."

The next day Bear rowed around in a bowl in the tub. He sang opera.

"Are you in Venice?" I asked.

"Yes," he said. "I'm a gondolier."

"The book is almost done," I said.

"*Va bene!*" said Bear.

The next day it rained, *again*.
Bear wore a beret and pretended he was in France.
"It always rains in Paris in spring, *mon cher*," he said.

"It's November," I said. "But guess what? I'm finished writing, the book is done. We can go on a real trip. Someplace sunny."

"I want to pick," he said.

Bear looked at all the maps.

"China?

Australia?

Sri Lanka?

Tahiti?"

Finally he folded up
the maps.

"Costa Rica," he said. "We're going to see a Cloud Forest."
"A Cloud Forest is a *RAIN* forest!" I said.
"We might see a quetzal," he said. "The most beautiful bird in the world."
"It lives in a *RAIN forest*," I yelled.

"We can hike through the jungle and everything," said Bear.

"The wet *RAINY jungle!*" I screamed.

"I'm glad you're excited," he said. "I am, too. We'll have a wonderful time."